# NOTES ON DRAGONS

## CHRISTOPHER BRAMLEY

First paperback edition printed 2015 in the United Kingdom
First e-book edition distributed 2014 from the United Kingdom

Copyright © 2014 Christopher Bramley.

The moral right of the author has been asserted.

All rights reserved.
No part of this book shall be stored, reproduced or transmitted in any form or by any means, electronic or mechanical, including photocopying, recording, or by any information retrieval system without written permission of the publisher, nor be otherwise circulated in any form or binding or cover other than that in which it is published and without a similar condition being imposed on the subsequent purchaser.

Published, Designed and Set by Sanctum Publishing
For all enquiries please contact local book providers or email:
info@sanctumpublishing.co.uk
All images, maps and other media Copyright © 2014 Sanctum Publishing
www.sanctumpublishing.co.uk

A CIP catalogue record for this book is available from the British Library.

ISBN 978-0-9931273-1-1

*Although every precaution has been taken in the preparation of this book, the publisher and author assume no responsibility for errors or omissions. Neither is any liability assumed for damages resulting from the use of this information contained herein. All characters in this publication are fictitious and any resemblance to real persons, living or dead, is purely coincidental.*

Dedicated to all those who dream of Dragons.

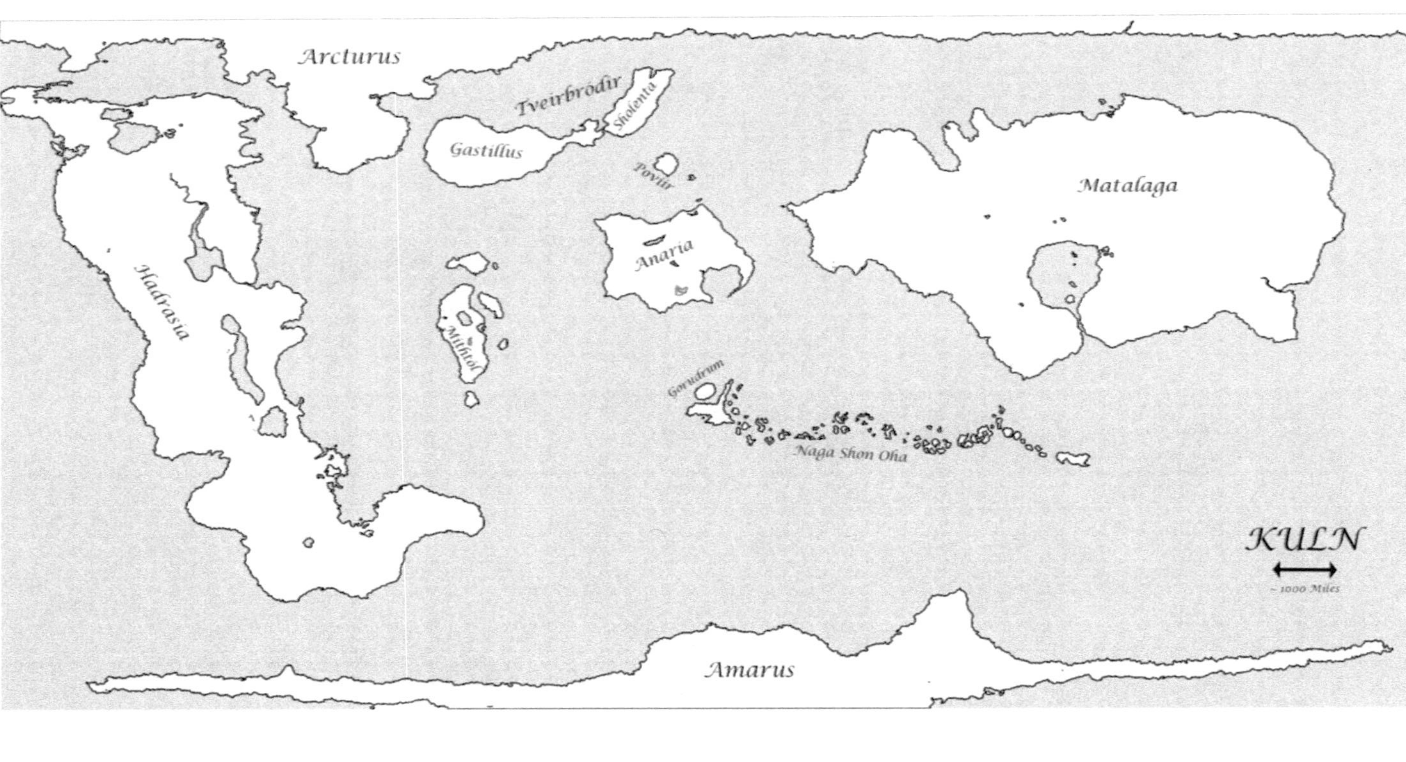

Arcturus
Tveirbrodir
Sholenia
Gastillus
Poviir
Matalaga
Anaria
Mithtol
Hadrasia
Gorudrum
Naga Shon Oha
KULN
~ 1000 Miles
Amarus

# Foreword and Acknowledgement

Dragons of all forms: for me, they are an eclectic mix of east and west. The godlike power and disposition, magic and intelligence of the east meets the raw brutal natural power and all-consuming flame of the west. The arrogance and might of Smaug, the honour and courage of Dragonheart, the charm and magic of R. Dragon, the mystery and disdain of those found in D&D, the fury of those in Skyrim; the wonderful and inventive Discworld dragons, the engineered and telepathic creatures of Anne McCaffrey, the mysterious dragons of eastern mythology and many more, as creatures they have always fascinated me.

Few other non-extant creatures exert such a powerful influence over many cultures and their languages and perceptions around the world. In some ways, they represent the pinnacle of our desires - the absolutes of beauty, freedom, flight, power, magic, and wealth.

This short companion book is for those who wonder how Dragons might exist; to understand those found in **The Serpent Calls** perhaps a little better; and for the fascination they have for Aldwyn, *mm, ah.*

*- CB, 2014*

# *Excerpt from Notes on Dragons*

All that follows is a collection of data from several sources: information in the most trusted older texts, research recorded during the (very regrettable) Drake Years, when scholars had a tragic but singular opportunity to study a dragon's anatomy firsthand; various current and past scientific experiment results; and from my own discussions with the great *Nāginī* Györnàeldàr. All these have led me to some quantifiable and interesting conclusions about how a creature like a Dragon can exist in nature. I do not believe, as some suggest, that they are a by-product of the chaotic influences rife in the Universe. They are fantastic creatures, and our current understanding of science should preclude the possibility of their existence. Nevertheless, they DO exist, and I have long been fascinated with them as a species.

Dragons are unique in a multiplicity of ways from any other being. Of all creatures, they have wings separate to their other limbs. They are not elongated ribs, nor are they modified arms such as birds or bats have, although they are closest in structure to the latter. Their wings are clawed appendages built specifically for flight, although they can be used for gripping (they can hold the Dragon's weight!) or slicing with the "wrist" tine, which is actually analogous to an incredibly strong thick prehensile thumb. So realistically, they are sextupeds, like the mythical centaurians (although I will not rule out their existence, given the creatures I have now seen). Few other creatures have six limbs that are not insects.

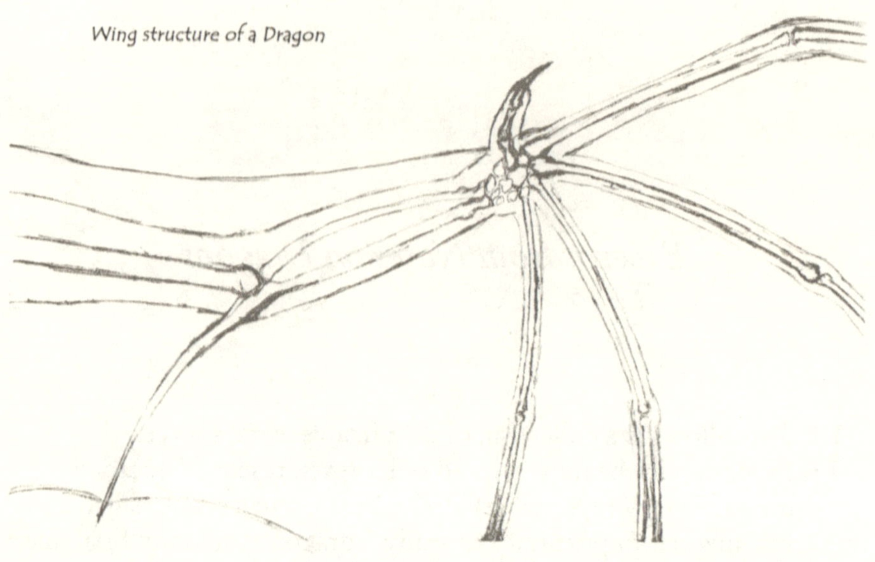

*Wing structure of a Dragon*

Their wings are wider than the Dragon's extended length, with a flexible wrist and arm that can be locked to provide gliding surfaces or folded in for faster, more agile flight. The membranes are spread by what appear to be long thick modified "fingers", which are incredibly flexible and surrounded by strong muscles which lend exceptional control. The Dragon's agility in the air is nothing short of astonishing. They can take off and land vertically, hover, and perform manoeuvres better reserved for a swallow. It seems they can adjust the surface area and lift edge to suit many needs. I have seen the Dragon glide slowly tens of feet above the ground - so slowly it seems she is about to drop from the air - but from what I understand, they can reach nearly forty thousand feet into the skies – beyond imagination! – if they are moving at speed substantial enough to provide lift in what I can only imagine as such thin air. Having seen Györnàeldàr move, and from remarks she has given, I estimate that in thin enough air at such heights, she can probably cover more than three hundred miles in one hour, and her stamina is such that she could perhaps circle the globe before resting if she so chose. In stooping she will be limited by the thicker air near the ground, but my best estimations suggest at most only one third slower than her top flight speed.

Why are they so large? Apart from being large by design, I also believe part of the answer, from the annals of our scholars, is equally simple. No feathers! Birds have to replace flight feathers, which can take a long time. Dragons do not. So bird size is limited by feather replacement time as well as weight. Therefore a bird would have to live a very long time to be very large. Dragons will live forever, barring accident, and are hardly small when born, or hatched. Györnàeldàr will not discuss that information with me for some reason - perhaps it is sacred to dragons, or considered inappropriate. They seem to have no real concept of time, something you can expect from an immortal. She will politely refer to "our" years for reference in discussions.

She has told me that Dragons grow slowly, but never stop, and that each is unique in form. From data available I estimate they grow roughly a foot for every thousand human years of life. This begins to slow gradually after the incredible number of around 200,000 years of life; she is roughly  250 feet long for an estimated 252, 000 years, although I do not know her size at "birth". The older and larger they get, the longer and more frequently they "slumber" - a term perhaps analogous to a hibernation of sorts – but conversely, the more and more powerful they become. Perhaps they simply weigh more and more heavily on reality. It is inferred that Dragons have other powers than simply those of flight, physical prowess, or even fire.

Györnàeldàr compared to average human

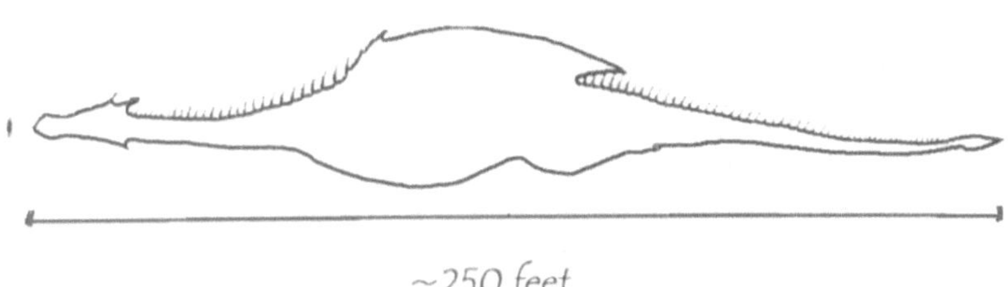

~250 feet

The numbers boggle the mind, and she has mentioned yet older Dragons. There are Elder Ones; the youngest of these is the only one currently awake, she says, and is circa 511, 000 years old, according to calculations making him roughly 320 feet long. The oldest might be a frankly inconceivable hundreds of millions of years old. A dragon of 'only' 5 million years might be in the region of 1200 feet long. That is a very conservative estimate for an old drake. It could be tens or hundreds of millions of years. Even Györnàeldàr does not know when the first of her kind emerged in the dawn of history; despite the slowing of their growth, this most ancient one would surely be the largest living creature on Kuln.

These things should not be possible, indeed cannot be with normal flesh and blood. Nothing should be so fast and agile at such sizes, nor live so long and grow so large. Yet I have seen their pinions able to support them in the air with my own eyes. Many have dismissed this as fantasy, citing that flesh and bone could not support the stresses that would be sustained hauling a forty-plus ton being into flight. However, it is precisely that fact which proves the point. Dragons are *not* built from a standard calcium-based skeleton and red muscle, as are we and most creatures on two – or four – legs. There are four identical organs, two in the back under the ribs and two in the abdomen around the kidneys, which have no analogues in other creatures and that I believe fill with hydrogen. This would lighten the Dragon and provide additional buoyancy, enough to allow the powerful muscles and bones to take the strain. These are lined with a thick mucus which would be excellent in slowing hydrogen loss, along with a return system in the body.

It seems that as Györnàeldàr states, even between individuals structure and appearance varies wildly. She is completely different in form to the young drake studied and recorded by men. Their skeletal structure is as different from other creatures as their flesh and other organs. The bones are reported to be incredibly light and strong. Our best scientific techniques and all our data have led us to believe they are apparently made of tiny tubes packed together tightly in a hollow matrix – possibly a carbon and calcium mix. They are flexible but rigid, and far stronger than any metal we can forge. The talons are solidly compressed from this material and are nearly as hard as diamond – certainly they can carve into solid rock with ease. The scales are light enough that one could be used as a shield with less than half the weight of equivalent steel, and with far better protection, yet they are all but impenetrable.

The flesh itself is incredibly dense, yet lean, accounting for their great strength, but it holds another secret. Dragons are not only immortal, possessing everlasting cell repair and growth, but they have astonishing regeneration as well. They can survive a wound that would kill any other creature, and heal it far quicker than you would think possible. The flesh does not just knit, but it actually regenerates. Even after the young dragon whose death began the Drake Years died, its body continued healing the ghastly wounds, confounding the attempts to dissect it for several days. Eventually only the scales show a mark, and that sheds in time. Their powers of repair are surpassed only by chaotic abominations (creatures that can typically only be destroyed by fire, or pure metals and plants). As long as they are alive, they will heal.

Their senses are quite extraordinary. Györnàeldàr saw in close detail humans battling creatures from something in the region of twenty thousand feet in the air, and can read script on a human-sized pendant from tens of feet away. Her eyes glow, very brightly, and evoke uncontrollable fear when fixed full upon you. I can only assume it is the strength of will of such an apex predator combined with the fearful intelligence behind the gaze, but simply being within her presence is frightening, although this lessens in time. She told me that they see clearly in total darkness. Certainly her eyes can light an entire campsite at night, a truly "burning gaze". She could hear our companions' heartbeats from more than sixty feet distant, and her sense of smell seems equally sharp. It is hard to take a dragon unawares!

The natural internal body heat of dragons is incredibly high. I have felt the heat emanating from our companion from many feet! Their internal heat seems to be usable as an energy source for long periods of time, perhaps sustaining them during "slumber", yet there seems to also be a regulatory function that prevents overheating. Perhaps the spines, horns and osteoderms they bear are capillary-loaded and extremely efficient at radiating heat, as in the Crocodilae family. The wings are certainly hot to the touch, and full of blood vessels. The membranes are vast, and must aid cooling considerably - or indeed heating, if they sun themselves. Györnàeldàr does enjoy sunning, but it cannot be for energy. They are certainly not cold blooded like reptiles, and despite possessing forked tongues and scales, they are akin to mammals as well. In fact, they have attributes from many other creatures apparent, and are truly separate from all other species. Their blood is volatile and hot, and also slightly acidic. It can mark human flesh, but ionic exchange is far greater when in contact with metals (mainly iron) or metal-bearing rock, where it will quickly react and generate heat. The hearts are large and four chambered, and pump the blood around the body at a tremendous pressure. It seems that they oxygenate their blood very efficiently, and it is thought a dragon could hold its breath for some considerable time if required.

These things aside, the most puzzling thing about these creatures is their ability to breathe flames from their mouths, and with considerable control. From observing flame types, and the notes from the old scripts, I believe that they use gases as a fuel source. Furthermore, after careful thought and research, as well as observing feeding habits and direct information from the dragon herself, I have concluded that they must use not one, but four different types. This meshes with the observational notes on the autopsy of the dragon's corpse that was performed at the start of the Drake Years.

I believe these gases are likely obtained from several sources. One is food and water through digestion; one is perhaps simply breathing; and the last is from consuming non-organic materials, which I have directly witnessed. Each stomach, of which there are three, seems to have a different function – extracting nutrients from the water they drink and the vast amounts of flesh they consume (you could not mistake Györnàeldàr for an herbivore. She is a supreme predator); separating chemicals from waste from the first stomach for other gases; and lastly rendering down inorganic materials for their components (one of these organs seems to be a "reaction stomach" with thicker walls and extremely powerful acids) to extract the chemicals required for flame.

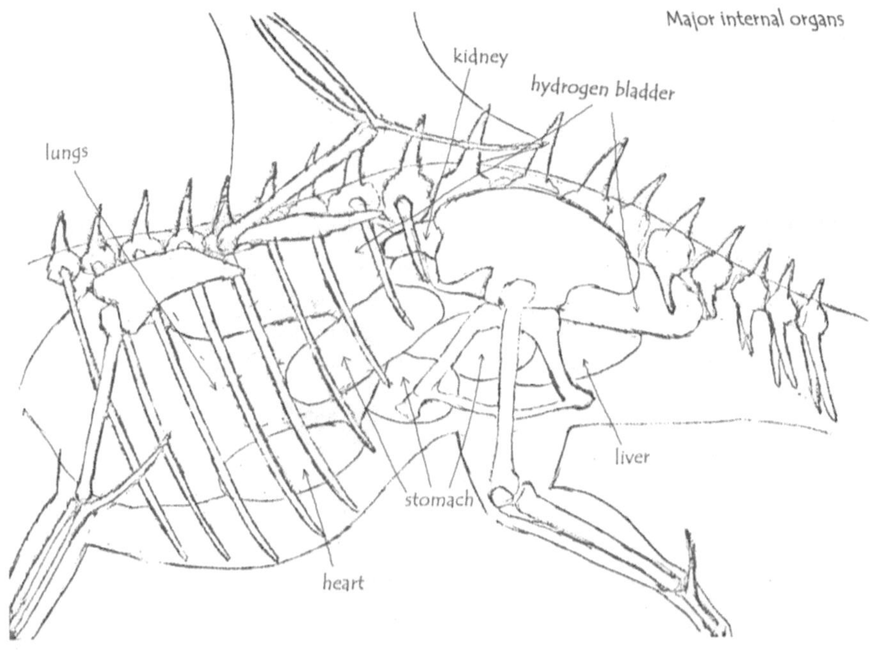


In the latter case, I am convinced the acid is for chemical reactions instead of digestion, as the fluid is capable of rendering down anything rapidly up to and including metals. It appears Dragons have an incredible sense of smell. Györnàeldàr can detect which rocks and soils contain the chemical elements she needs to ingest for hotter flames, and it is possible that she unconsciously adjusts it in response to chemical indicators in the rock ingested.  Food is broken down by the powerful digestive system very rapidly and processed in a short gut common to most pure carnivores. Their multiple stomachs have a natural constricting motion in addition to the acids, and the stomachs and bowels have a very thick lining composed of different tissue layers. Each one seems to be able to capture a type of molecule, in this case gas, and transport it. The gases produced are drawn to large pressured sacks or bladders, heavily lined with thick mucus which slows the loss of gas through the bladder walls. Methane, hydrogen and oxygen are gained from organic food and water, with the latter two also perhaps filtered from breathing; the fourth I can only guess to be acetylene, or cyanogen. Dragons seem to be immune to poisons, as they will eat minerals heavy in cyanides. Either may give the basis for the creation of cyanogens or acetylene.

On the subject of methane in digestion, Dragon excrement is sulphur and carbon-heavy, and very acidic when fresh, but dry and rock-like shortly after excretion. The moisture is mainly external to the stool, perhaps to aid in excreting. One curious anomaly is that they expel no gas from the rear apart from almost pure sulphur wastes, as their bodies are geared towards the aforementioned processing of flammable gases internally into the components for their flame. Dragons produce surprisingly little excrement. Their bodies are extremely efficient systems.

Without food, rock/minerals, and water, or if overused, a Dragon will eventually run out of flame and need to recharge all reservoirs. I would not consider this a great disadvantage, given their physical prowess, but they seem very conscientious at ensuring they are ever-filled.

There is an organic exhalation valve – a second one-way trachea – which can allow a lungful of air, drawn in to the (extremely large) lungs normally, to be redirected through this valve at varying pressures derived from lung contraction on exhalation. This seems an act of will. The dragon can close either airway, possibly of use against contamination or water.

Sealable, directional cone-like sphincters in the walls of the valve direct a high-pressure stream of pure gas from one or more of the four large pressurised reservoirs (using dense powerfully contracting muscles, of which they have many!) at adjustable quantities into the air stream, allowing a flame that can be wide, long, and low temperature, or very finely controlled in a shorter focused jet that can melt or even vaporise rock. Experiments have shown that the dragon can consciously decide the form of flame, and will mix varying streams of gas. Only on the lower temperature flames will the dragon also breathe out hard, as this gives vast impetus to the flame, but will contaminate it with carbon monoxide and nitrogen, reducing the burn efficiency.

## Representation of Dragon throat and gas system

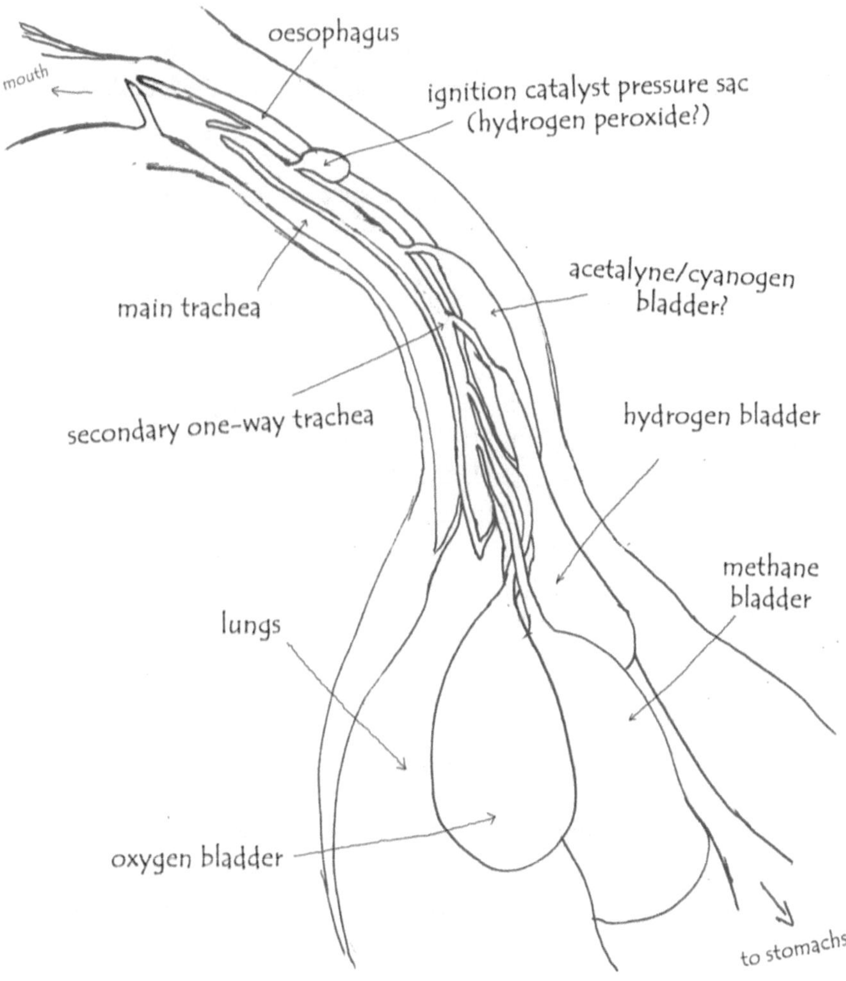


The hottest flame produced is, I believe, a mix of pure oxygen and either acetylene or cyanogens. Whatever the composition, it is exponentially hotter than any flame produced by man, and can cut through anything it encounters with impunity. Rock and steel can be melted or vaporised, and even power-laced creations of the mystics and the grey-silver mithríl (which I believe is a titanium alloy) that forms lighter and harder than steel will be quickly consumed. This flame, however, is the weakest in blast effect, and the least used, being most limited in reservoir. The bladder for this gas is the smallest and is part-filled with some form of strong natural solvent, perhaps half or more, which probably mixes with the acetylene or equivalent to help stabilise it - an indicator perhaps of pressure limitations and/or gas availability.

Flames change colours as hydrogen is added or substituted, producing a cooler and less visible but cleaner flame. Györnàeldàr assures me that she has used this underwater in brief bursts! I am not sure what application this has for her. I imagine this is again pressure related, as hydrogen, I believe, should be able to be stored at much higher pressure than a cyanide-derived gas. When the dragon uses hydrogen and oxygen, it can extend the flame much further, as oxygen is a bigger bladder at an even greater pressure. Hydrogen is also redirected by the body to the four large bladders above and below the lungs of course, but these are not linked to the hydrogen flame bladder.

When methane is injected into the air stream the dragon usually augments this with less pure oxygen and more a balance of air from the lungs. The more lung air used over bladder pressure, the more yellow-orange the flame due to carbon monoxide. With the enormous power of the lungs behind them, these more typical yellow flames can be many times the length of the dragon,  but are not comparatively hot (i.e. enough to melt steel), although they will ignite wood and burn flesh easily enough. They do, however, have the added pressure to bowl creatures over, exposing more surface area to the flame, and seem to be the most plentiful of the gas types, being the easiest to extract. The bladder for methane is very large indeed! There is no odorous breath from the methane (Scholars believe that it is the sulphur in flatulence that smells bad).

All of these flames seem to use oxygen in a pure delivered form in the throat as the oxidiser with heat, and even with a mixture of all the gases for a truly analogue flame; however, if required for whatever reason, the Dragon can simply use air from the throat. This would produce far feebler results, and might result in flames being extinguished if there is too much carbon monoxide and not enough oxygen left. Perhaps this is why their flames are reported to get weaker after extended use.

The lungs are much proportionately larger and drier than usual in animals, and hot, reducing the moisture exhaled. The moisture drawn in from breathing is collected by a "condenser palate" and absorbed. The oral flesh itself is tough and very impervious to temperature, and is also coated in a transparent, thin, and constantly replenishing mucus that is extremely non-heat conductive.  The mouth is typically held wide open when fire-breathing so that even low temperature flames do not lick the flesh or teeth. Fine control of the throat muscles and "lips" means that the focused higher temperature flames will not touch either. Györnàeldàr in fact appears to burn the higher temperature flames from just past her lips by igniting a stream of purer gases and immediately contracting her throat and controlling her mouth shape so that the gas only burns outside. It is extraordinary to watch.

The last of the great questions then is: How do they ignite the flame? For the majority of sentients this involves heat derived from a spark or ember. Some esteemed colleagues have suggested that they have mineral teeth which can produce sparks, which I think ridiculous – quite apart from lack of any evidence in the dissected Dragon! – whilst others assume that they can generate electrical arcs in their throats, which would be uncomfortable and dangerous. The ionisation of air is believed to be quite damaging to mucous membranes (of which there are many in a throat). In fact Dragons have a far more reliable – and scientifically sound! – approach. There is a separate bladder in the throat, a tiny extremely thick-walled chamber situated further up the neck at the top of the second trachea, that produces what I believe is concentrated hydrogen peroxide and holds it under very high pressure. This decomposes into hot gases rapidly, which fill the chamber. Dragons can spray these hot gases in a controlled stream into other gases exhaled - most likely acetylene or cyanogens for the low ignition point - for initial oxidation and spontaneous combustion. This is instinctive and very reliable. Then oxygen and other gas quantities can be adjusted to suit for desired flame type. Ignition can occur in a fraction of a second, a truly remarkable biological development; perhaps similar in nature to the fat beetles of Matalaga that can expel an acidic, boiling liquid at will from their anus to blind predators.

There is, too, something more to these flames than mere heat. Dragons seem able to tap into a plane of energy we theorise as *dark energy* and impart some *other* power into the flames. Györnàeldàr has also spoken of being able to manipulate this energy in other ways; it is something a dragon naturally perceives within our universe, but mere humans cannot unless by chance of birth or training, and then only dimly. This may explain why some beings can wield powers that the uneducated would term *magic.* I myself have a very basic understanding of this all-pervading energy from my time studying with the *Daktarim,* and how to use it to encourage a human body to heal more quickly and effectively.

So I am satisfied, as a scientist, that Dragons can and do exist. And yet, despite all my cogitations on the matter, they remain a mystery. How did they develop these traits? What could make something like this exist? Did they evolve? Perhaps they do use acetylene, or even cyanogens, as their hottest flame base – but how do they get it from the rock? It cannot only be one method of chemical extraction, else they would be bound only to areas that had that element. Do they break down or react elements into hydrogen cyanide, then oxidised over nitrogen dioxide formed from nitric oxide, and somehow mixed with copper salts? That seems an awfully complex solution, and yet it is the simplest one to hand. Most other ways of obtaining these gases are complex and unable to fit properly within the scope of a physical body, even that of a Dragon, in any way I can see.

Likewise, the analysis of their bones and muscles still does not explain how they form it, if it is even anything like normal flesh and bone. When a Dragon dives, the wings should be torn off, no matter how strong and flexible, but they can reach terminal velocity and then snap their wings open, catching hundreds of feet of air with controlled finesse. They heal wounds that are beyond all survivability for other life. Their cells regenerate and replenish indefinitely, but they do not know disease or mutation. They can crack rock and stone with their very limbs! So even for their size, they have incredible strength. Their power to weight ratio is far in excess of what you would expect for such a huge being. All of the above hypotheses notwithstanding, they are perhaps somewhat outside the realms of our reality.

I believe that they are partly Other, not totally bound without our limited set of dimensions. I think they are beings of several planes of existence, perhaps inhabiting to a lesser degree the levels of energy occupied by the Gods. Their will is strong enough to affect other creatures, other events, through observation. So can they manipulate what we see as bound reality to a greater degree than we? They remain, as mentioned, a great mystery, but there is no doubt that in combination, their senses, armour, dense flesh and bone structure, and their ability to transcend the understood laws of flame - and indeed science - have produced the most incredible marvel of nature: a creature that is relatively light, strong, fast, and fully eternal, with great powers of healing and flight, the ability to wield unearthly powers, and an intellect to match. Truly they are the pinnacle of existence, immortal and immutable, which can explain the awe – and jealousy – of humans. I suspect we will never truly understand them.

# *Excerpt from On Draconic Culture*

*L*ittle is known of their culture, bar the cerebral elite's reluctant admission that dragons are probably the most learned creatures on this planet. This pains me a little to say, having dedicated my life to study! Yet I have been complimented on my knowledge by a Dragon, and it was the greatest accolade I have received. They remember everything perfectly, and understand and learn quickly; they can replicate, if they care enough, most of the feats of the sentient races... but they have little need. They require no shelter, no clothes; they are living weapons, impervious and unchanging. They are erudite, and love to discourse and think. They can be arrogant and aloof, but I challenge you to live forever in the greatest avatar possible to a life form and not feel overly confident at times! The intelligence of Dragons is quite alien to humans, but it cannot be denied. Those who dismiss them merely as destructive animals are very misinformed.

Their language is ancient and complex. It is possible for a human to speak it in a limited fashion, but never with the correct tonal sounds (or full range of pitch). Too, it is often excessively formal and dignified. They refer to themselves as "Zhōng Gúorén Huáng dì Nāgāra", which means "The Dragon People of the Kingdom of Earth and Heaven". This is sometimes shortened to Nāgāra, taken to mean Dragons (more literally Serpents, but I would recommend not referring to them as such, and calling one "Wyrm" is asking for death). All of them are considered nobility – the honorifics Nāgā and Nāgìnī both mean "Majesty", as if addressing royalty, or respectively "Lord" and "Lady". It is wise to remember that they are a proud race that expects respect from other "lesser" races. To insult a Dragon is a foolish thing, and they do not tolerate fools lightly.

The dragons refer to Arkhe, the Creator of Existence, the Grandfather if you like of the "Great Dragons", their greater kin (or so I am told). In their belief, Arkhe created the universe, and the worlds within. The worlds brought forth their homage to Him in the form of lesser Gods, beings of great power that could see and feel the great dark threads binding existence, connecting them to everything. These "Lesser Gods" are what they call the Great Dragons. The will of these beings is so great, and their weight on the planes of existence so high, that they appear to have an effect remarked upon, oddly,  in the newer quantum theories in The Sanctum. They postulate that observation changes the Universe by the smallest amount, but the Dragons believe that what the great Dragons dream is reality, and that they Dream the World. This might suggest that they manipulate the Space-Time Continuum on an observational-belief basis - that they perhaps weigh so heavily on reality that they can consciously affect it at a noticeable level, making them truly powerful (should they be real).

As to the physical makeup of the Great Dragons, which are alluded to in ancient texts, and spoken of sparingly in my discussions with our Draconic friend, I can only guess that they are as different from a Dragon as a Dragon is from us. They do not appear bound completely to the physical laws within which we all dwell. Their fire is not chemical in nature from all accounts, as is even the hottest of Dragon-fire, but I guess to be a form of plasma, generated in some fashion from the *dark energy* of the universe (which does exist! I will miss Draef's irritation on that count). Perhaps they merely transmute its state into light and heat, but it appears to have more properties than that, acting perhaps as the conduit for the Great Dragon's Dream state and the Physical world. It may be that the flame is what they use to bridge planes between differing energy levels and effect their will upon the world.

What I am told, and I cannot believe through hearsay, is that a Great Dragon can be so many thousands of feet as to be leagues – leagues! – in length. It would dwarf even the most ancient of the Dragons! A Dragon greater than most cities is something I cannot countenance. Although I have seen many wonders in my research, a single organism the size of mountains seem ridiculous. My suspicions are that either they are the usual Dragons – impressive enough! – seen by excitable eye, or that the Dragons have created themselves a form of gods in their own image, as every sentient race we know of has.

Now THAT is something I shall have to research, if I ever find time in this life! I will never be able to consider the Dragons, Györnàeldàr especially, as "lesser".

– Aldwyn Varelin

Emergence of a Greater Dragon?

# About the Author

Chris lives in Surrey in the UK. During the day he labours under the guise of a Technical Consultant and Trainer in IT, but the rest of the time he is equally busy writing, avidly reading, working out, practicing martial arts, rock climbing, and playing the odd game here and there. He is also a lazy musician and artist, roughly able to tell one end from another of about five instruments and occasionally drawing decently, and enjoys fixing things, researching, and generally getting stuff done. He loves to learn new things and teach others whatever subjects he knows enough about, and is full of generally useless facts. Fantasy, Sci-Fi and books have been a staple for countless years, and he is as avid a follower of Lord of the Rings and its ilk as he is a complete Star Wars geek. Sometimes he sleeps.

You can follow him on Twitter (**@christopbramley**) or Facebook, or visit **www.christopherbramley.co.uk** for updates on this and his other novels.

www.ingramcontent.com/pod-product-compliance
Lightning Source LLC
Chambersburg PA
CBHW021027120726

47905CB00009B/3218